W9-AAT-812

Monsters
and Mythical Creatures

Trolls

Other titles in the Monsters and Mythical Creatures series include:

Aliens
Cyclops
Demons
Dragons
Frankenstein
Goblins
Medusa
The Mummy
Water Monsters
Zombies

Monsters

and Mythical Creatures

Trolls

Gail B. Stewart

ReferencePoint
Press®

San Diego, CA

© 2012 ReferencePoint Press, Inc.
Printed in the United States

For more information, contact:
ReferencePoint Press, Inc.
PO Box 27779
San Diego, CA 92198
www.ReferencePointPress.com

LIBRARY OF CONGRESS CATALOGING-IN-PUBLICATION DATA

Stewart, Gail B. (Gail Barbara), 1949–
  Trolls / by Gail Stewart.
      p. cm. — (Monsters and mythical creatures series)
  Includes bibliographical references and index.
  ISBN-13: 978-1-60152-183-5 (hardback)
  ISBN-10: 1-60152-183-9 (hardback)
  1. Trolls—Juvenile literature. I. Title. II. Series.
  GR555.S94 2012
  398.21—dc23
                                                    2011016391

Contents

Trolls on the Prowl

Two brothers, Erik and Peter, are walking through a deep forest not far from their little home in central Norway. Aged 7 and 10, the boys are the oldest of seven children, and because their family is very poor, their parents have sent them out into the world to beg for food. At first they are excited by the adventure of traveling on their own and eager to see the world beyond their tiny rural home, but after a while they start to feel uneasy.

The sudden silence suggests that something is wrong. Only moments before, the morning was alive with sound. From the lowing of cattle and occasional barks of the farm dogs on the hills below to the singing of birds and the hum of insects, everything seemed normal. However, as quickly as if someone threw a switch, all sounds disappeared. And just as it occurs to them what such silence may mean, the ground beneath them begins to rumble and shake. As the boys know from hearing their parents' warnings, that sudden silence almost certainly signals what all of their neighbors fear most: Trolls are on the prowl.

Within a few minutes, the boys realize that all hope is lost. Cowering behind a tree, they watch as two gigantic trolls stumble into the clearing. The creatures are horrid to look at—each has three heads and long, sharp teeth. The odor that comes off their skin is almost unbearably foul. Using their own keen sense of smell, the trolls spot Erik and Peter within seconds. They pick up the terrified brothers as if they are rag dolls, plunge them into a large sack,

and take them back to their troll-home. There the boys will be fat-
tened up until they are fit to eat.

Smelly, Ugly, and Flesh Hungry

So begins one of hundreds of folktales about trolls. According to
these tales, trolls are the most frightening of all creatures on the
earth. They vary in size and appearance—one type is small enough
to fit in a child's mitten, while most are so gigantic that they tower
above the tallest pines. Some have one head, while others may have
as many as 12. And while a very few trolls can be merely mischievous
rather than mean, the majority of trolls—especially those who live in
the sea, the mountains, and the dense, dark forests—are exceptionally dangerous.

In the Erik and Peter tale, the boys are confronted by full-grown
mountain trolls, most of which are said to be the size of five large
men—or even larger. Their bulbous eyes are the size of pot lids, and
their noses are often so long that
when they are cooking a meal,
they must first tuck their noses
into their belts to keep them out
of the stewpot. Finally, as the two
boys learn firsthand, the stink of a
troll is almost more than a human
can bear. "In some of the stories
my grandfather used to tell us,
the smell coming off some trolls
ranged from that of the most vile, smelly old socks to the stench of
a barn that has not been cleaned in years," notes native Norwegian
Inez Knutsen. "And that can be just a few minutes after that troll has
been bathed!"[1]

Even more intimidating than a troll's size, however, is its ferocious nature. Unlike the giants and ogres that are prominent in the
folktales of England, Germany, and other areas of Europe, trolls
are rarely kindly or sympathetic characters. Most trolls are violent
and loathe humans and their societies. To a troll, a human is good
for one thing only—a meal. While trolls in stories may choose to

Did You Know?

When hungry enough,
some legends say, trolls will
eat other trolls—making
them one of the few canni-
balistic creatures in folklore.

A huge troll ventures from its forest hideaway to spy on a nearby village in this John Bauer illustration from around 1913.

speak politely to a human, their actions belie any civility, notes Steve Benson, a scholar of Scandinavian studies.

> They're nasty, mean, and without any redeeming characteristics whatsoever. They seem happiest when they are terrorizing humans—stealing their cattle, imprisoning their children, and generally frightening anyone in the vicinity. So many of the troll tales illustrate this—they are the ancient equivalent of the worst sort of bully. Physical and verbal abuse is what they are best at. That is simply the nature of trolls.[2]

"Who Better than a Troll?"

Most of what is known about the legendary trolls comes from centuries-old folktales of Norway, though other Scandinavian countries, including Sweden, Iceland, and Denmark, have created troll stories, too. In addition to appearing in those old tales, trolls have appeared in more recent literature—from J.R.R. Tolkien's *Lord of the Rings* to J.K. Rowling's *Harry Potter and the Sorcerer's Stone*. They are featured in the classical music of Norwegian composer Edvard Grieg as well as in a variety of twenty-first-century role-playing and video games.

Did You Know?

In one tale a troll is so large he catches a whale, puts it on a stringer, and carries it home for dinner.

Those who are familiar with the many troll legends are not at all surprised to see the creatures surfacing in more contemporary books, movies, and other forms of entertainment. "After all," says Benson, "when you come right down to it, and you need a really, really bad guy for a story— who better than a troll?"[3]

Chapter 1

A Long Legacy of Trouble

As is true with most legends, it is impossible to trace the origin of troll tales with complete accuracy. However, folklore experts believe that the first troll stories were told in what is now Norway by some of the earliest settlers there. By the ninth century—and perhaps even earlier—people were hearing and repeating the stories, which were often in the form of poetic verse.

It was early in the ninth century that a traveling minstrel named Bragi Boddason, famous for entertaining kings and queens, recounted an unusual story. He told of an encounter with a female troll who describes herself and her fellow trolls as primitive, destructive, and ravenously hungry. The following is an English translation of Boddason's Old Norse version of what the troll-wife (as she was known) says:

> They call me Troll;
> Gnawer of the Moon,
> Giant of the Gale-blasts,
> Curse of the rain-hall,
> Companion of the Sibyl,
> Nightroaming hag,
> Swallower of the loaf of heaven.
> What is a Troll but that?[4]

An Origin in Toes

According to ancient Norse folklore, trolls are part of a group of creatures known as dark beings, which are the embodiment of evil—and trolls are the most evil of all. Norse legends say that to understand how trolls and the other dark beings came into existence, it is necessary to go back to the Frost Giants, beings who existed before the universe itself.

Ymir was the first Frost Giant, a monster with six heads and six arms. He was murdered by three brothers who used his body to create the physical universe. From Ymir's blood came the seas and rivers, and from his skull came the sky. His bones became mountains, his teeth boulders, and from between his toes crawled the race of trolls.

The members of the troll race were not social. Instead, they preferred the privacy of dark places—some lived in the mountains, others stayed within forests, and many lived underground or underwater. In these secret domains, they plotted evil and mischief. Trolls were especially hostile to human beings, for they considered them interlopers. According to troll folklore specialist Joanne Asala, the trolls' fury began to simmer soon after the Ice Age glaciers melted. "When the glacier retreated, human tribes from the south moved into the newly uncovered territory and named it Norway," says Asala. "They considered themselves the first inhabitants, but they soon discovered they were wrong. The trolls believed that everything surrounding their home belonged to them. . . . They hated it when men cleared forests and planted crops."[5]

Did You Know?

Native people of Lapland (the northernmost parts of Finland and Sweden) once believed that trolls could turn themselves into bears.

The Self-Contained Society

Experts say there are several reasons why troll tales have not only survived since ancient times, but have flourished. One important reason is the structure of Norwegian society long ago.

For centuries after Norway was settled, it consisted almost exclusively of farms. There were no cities or large towns as there were in more southern parts of Europe; mostly there were large farms on which a great number of peasants lived and worked. Peasants, known as cotters, were granted small plots of land as payment for their work. On this land they could grow their family's food. Because of the rural setting, and because of the large number of workers, these large farms were more like remote, self-contained villages, according to historian Florence Ekstrand:

> All the food was raised and processed [on these farms], all the clothes and essentials were made here. Leather was tanned, horses shod, furniture built, candles dipped, wool and flax grown, prepared and woven. A large farm might have its own smith, builder, shoemaker, butcher, all in addition to farm hands, dairy maids, house maids and elderly relatives who called the place home.[6]

Troll tales abounded on these farms. Folklorists agree that the long, frigid, dark winters contributed to the popularity of such tales. Stories of wicked trolls helped pass the time, and the youngsters who shivered as they listened committed their favorite tales to memory and would repeat them years later to their own children.

Trolls and the Landscape

Another reason that troll tales flourished in the northernmost regions of Europe was the easy connection between the stories and the rough Norse terrain. As any child knew from the tales, an aversion to sunlight is one of the few weaknesses to afflict most trolls. That is why the creatures stay hidden during daylight hours and move about in the dark of night. Even a tiny glimpse of the sun will turn the biggest, fiercest troll to stone, and sometimes it may crack into thousands of pieces.

One popular tale shows what can happen to trolls who get careless about staying in the dark. According to this story, a young lad knows that he is in danger of being taken prisoner by a particularly hungry pair of trolls. Knowing that they will likely eat him unless he

"Look! There's a Troll"

Author Lise Lunge-Larsen says that many Norwegian parents still enjoy telling troll stories to their children and often use the physical landscape as a jumping-off place for a tale. One of her own most vivid childhood memories is from a time when she was just three years old and walking in the woods with her mother.

> We ambled along the trail in the dark, old growth forest filled with filtered sunlight, when my mother suddenly grabbed my arm and whispered, "Look! There's a troll." I actually thought my last moment had come, until I saw where she pointed: to a dead troll that had turned into an overturned tree root. Together we examined the troll, found his nose, arms, and even his eye sockets. It was a magical moment and to this day I point out all the dead trolls to my own children and their friends: A huge rock pile is a troll that burst, a tree root lying on its side is an ancient troll, and an oddly-shaped rock may be part of a nose.

Lise Lunge-Larsen, *The Troll with No Heart in His Body and Other Tales of Trolls from Norway.* Boston: Houghton Mifflin, 1999, pp. 6–7.

can escape, the boy begins to tell the trolls an exciting story featuring trolls as brave heroes. As he weaves the tale, he notices that glimmers of dawn are showing pink in the sky—and he keeps talking, hoping the trolls will not notice.

Mesmerized by the boy's story, the trolls pepper him with questions, and he continues to make up more stories. The boy tells them about how wealthy these trolls have become, and he taunts his two captors by telling them that they will never have a piece of gold as big as the trolls in his story have. When the two demand that the boy tell them the location of this huge piece of gold, he points behind them. The instant the trolls turn around to look, they are caught by the rising sun, and with a loud crack they are turned into stone.

Constant Reminders

Because of such tales, it did not take much imagination to look at the odd shapes in the hills and rocky outcroppings of Norway and see the faces of ugly trolls that had been turned to stone by the sun. Large piles of smaller stones could easily be one of these unfortunate trolls whose body had burst into thousands of pieces. Many Norwegian landmarks became closely associated with troll stories. The stones, petrified tree roots, and strangely shaped boulders constantly reminded Norwegians of the ugly creatures who were said to have inhabited the far north thousands of years before humans ever set foot there.

With just a little imagination, the rocky outcroppings and misshapen hills of Norway (pictured) suggest the presence of trolls long ago turned to stone by the sun.

The stone crags called Trold-Tindterne, or Peaks of the Trolls, in central Norway are said to be the scene of a bloody battle thousands of years ago between two bands of trolls. The battle had begun in twilight and was still raging as dawn approached. But the two armies were so engaged in the fight that they did not notice the sun coming up. As a result, the first rays of the sun suddenly turned both armies into rocks, which are still visible today.

According to some tales, even living trolls can be mistaken for rocks and hills. Many of the largest mountain trolls are so big that pine trees grow from the topsoil covering their neck and shoulders. When they shamble out of their dens after sunset, they look very much like the craggy mountains around them.

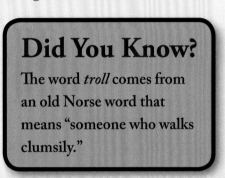

Did You Know?

The word *troll* comes from an old Norse word that means "someone who walks clumsily."

A Tradition of Belief

Such visual cues in the landscape only reinforced the unquestioning Norse belief in trolls. The first Christian missionaries began arriving in Norway early in the tenth century to spread the word of a gentle, loving, forgiving God, but they could not shake the Norse fascination with trolls.

While the concept of a gentle God held little appeal for these people who lived a hardscrabble existence in a place with an unforgiving climate half the year, they were intrigued by the idea of the devil, according to Asala. With his cloven hooves and his vindictive nature, the devil fit in more with the folklore of Norway, and instead of referring to him as "Satan" or "the devil," the Norse people named him "Old Eric." Writes Asala, "Some storytellers say that this devilish creature is closely related to the trolls, and perhaps may be master of them all."[7]

But the church in Rome was determined to convert the Norse people and officially banned the old superstitions—including the troll tales. However, the priests who actually lived among the Norse people were willing to take a less rigid view. They saw nothing terribly wrong with their parishioners keeping the old tales alive. Notes

Ekstrand, "As long as the Mass was celebrated, the gospel preached, the sacraments administered and the tithe collected, the fisher-folk and dairy maids could tell their old tales around the fire and little harm was done."[8]

Satisfied with this arrangement, the Norwegians went to church on Sundays, but many still enjoyed the traditional troll tales. Historians say that during this period some of the old stories became entwined with Christian symbolism. For example, one story involves a man named Heide who defeats a troll by drawing a ring around it and making the sign of the cross. As a result, the troll is doomed, glued to that spot forever.

The Trolls Fight Back

Christianity introduced new ideas and practices to an old, established way of life, and the troll stories reflected concern about these changes. From the earliest stories, listeners knew that trolls resented the coming of humans after the Ice Age. Later stories left the clear impression that the trolls saw the building of churches as yet another irritation. According to the tales, it was not only the bustle of human activity near the churches, but the tolling of the church bells that was particularly disturbing to the trolls.

> ### Did You Know?
> Some Scandinavian parents warn their children that they are behaving like "little trolls" when they are being naughty.

Stories began to include scenes of trolls hurling gigantic boulders down a mountainside toward a church. Today many churches throughout Scandinavia have huge rocks nearby, lending credibility to the legend. For example, in Denmark, a troll furious with the loud ringing of the bells is said to have thrown a boulder that was 39 feet (12m) high and weighed 1,000 tons (907 metric tons) at the church early one Sunday morning 500 years ago. The boulder came close, but the church was not hit; both rock and church still stand there today.

The Revenge of Lake Vättern?

Another of the talented illustrators of troll stories was John Bauer, who was born in 1882 and grew up near Lake Vättern in central Sweden. Many believed that trolls had once prowled the lake's shores and even lived within its deep waters. Even during Bauer's lifetime the lake was considered a treacherous body of water known for sudden, ferocious storms. Rarely would a year go by without someone drowning in the lake.

While Theodor Kittelsen and Erik Werenskiold illustrated the Norwegian troll tales, Bauer did illustrations for the Swedish ones. His trolls were ugly and hulking but not as frightening as Kittelsen's—a difference that matched the Swedish version of trolls very well. Bauer was a young man at the height of his career when he, his wife, and their two-year-old son were traveling on a steamer on the lake on a dark November night. A sudden storm arose and the boat capsized; all those on board drowned. "Around the Vattern, people shook their heads," writes Florence Ekstrand. "The trolls, they said, had taken their revenge."

Quoted in Florence Ekstrand, *Norwegian Trolls and Other Tales.* Seattle: Welcome, 1990, p. 31.

The trolls' dislike of religion in these stories is often apparent in another way. In some tales, trolls who suspect a human is nearby often sniff suspiciously (their noses are exceedingly sensitive). While in some of the tales, a troll declares that it smells human blood, in many other versions it identifies the blood it smells as Christian. In the tale "Soria Moria Castle," for example, when a huge troll comes bursting into the front door where a princess and a boy named Havor are hiding, it roars: "Ugh! Ugh! Ugh! Here I smell the blood of a Christian man!"[9]

A Threat to the Trolls

Though there was a bending of the rules while the priests ran the churches in Scandinavian countries, things changed drastically after the Protestant Reformation, when Lutheranism became the official branch of Christianity in the region. Not only were the Christian traditions of the last five centuries erased, but the old tales tolerated by the priests were outlawed. "[Martin] Luther wasn't tolerant of the old ways," notes Steve Benson. "The idea of those spirits, witches, trolls—all of that was intolerable. So troll stories really went out of favor then. Instead of the exciting stories of Odin, Thor, and those old gods, things were more modern—the Trinity. Not the old gods, not the trolls or the dwarves or any more of [such creatures]."[10]

But the most powerful threat to the tradition of troll stories was not religion, but rather the Industrial Revolution. In the mid-nineteenth century many of the people who had been living and working on the large farms moved to the cities to work shifts in factories that mass-produced goods that had previously been made by hand. That changed not only the economic structure of Norway but the social structure as well. The frigid winter nights were no longer spent sitting around the fire listening to troll tales. Says Ekstrand, "The long evenings of carding and spinning and story telling were gone; the wife of even a small farmer could now buy cloth woven in mills. The stories were stilled."[11]

A Treasure Rescued

Those changes could easily have spelled the end of the troll tales. The reliance on storytellers for entertainment had lessened substantially by the time of the Industrial Revolution. The old stories that had once provided so much enjoyment began to seem silly and childish to people eager for modernization.

It was the work of two remarkable young Norwegians in the mid-nineteenth century that rescued the trolls from their slow death. Peter Asbjornsen and Jorgen Moe were both interested in folktales. As a government naturalist, Asbjornsen spent much of his time tramping around the countryside and was able to visit the remote areas where some of the large old farms still stood. Some of the farmers Asbjornsen met were reluctant at first to talk about the troll tales, but his genuine enthusiasm for the old tales convinced some of the residents to share what they remembered. Explains Ekstrand: "Asbjornsen . . . [would] persuade the old cook of the estate or the grandmother of the house to tell him stories of the area. It was not always easy. Old people who were full of old folklore hesitated to tell it to strangers for fear of being taken for fools. But the sensitivity that shows in Asbjornsen's writing must have won their confidence, for the stories flowed."[12]

Moe also spent a great deal of time in rural Norway as a private tutor. He used many of his weekends and vacations talking to older people across the countryside and collected as many of

Brothers Jacob and Wilhelm Grimm listen to and write down fairy tales for their famous collection, as depicted in this painting from the late 1800s. Two Norwegians decided to follow their example; they compiled the folktales of Norway—many of which featured trolls.

the troll tales as he could find. The two friends decided to do what brothers Jacob and Wilhelm Grimm had done with the traditional German fairy tales. Asbjornsen and Moe published a compilation of the old folktales of Norway, called *Norske Folkevntyr (Norwegian Folktales)* in 1845 and followed it with a second volume in 1852. Readers loved the stories, and the Grimm brothers hailed the books as a masterpiece—high praise coming from the most famous collectors and writers of European folktales. Many felt the tales were enhanced by the writing style, which the authors purposely kept in the same simple, direct language of those who had recited them.

Illustrating Trolls

The success of those early volumes convinced Asbjornsen and Moe to publish an illustrated volume of their tales, which they did in 1877. The first artist to add pen-and-ink drawings to accompany the stories was Erik Werenskiold. Subsequent books were illustrated by another young artist named Theodor Kittelsen.

In a letter to the authors written around 1881, Werenskiold explained that Kittelsen seemed to understand the nature of trolls better than anyone he had ever met. "Kittelsen has a wild, individual, inventive fantasy," Werenskiold wrote. "For many years I have had the constant thought that he should be the man to do that side of your [adventures] which none of the rest of us has yet been able to accomplish, namely the purely fantastic creations!"[13]

When Asbjornsen saw Kittelsen's sketches for the first time, he was both impressed and shocked. Though the drawings were stunning in their detail, Kittelsen's depiction of the trolls was very scary and vivid, and Asbjornsen was unsure whether such art would be too frightening for children. However, his reservations were unfounded. Readers loved the book with its haunting tales illustrated by the combined art of Kittelsen and Werenskiold, and the volume was hailed as one of Norway's treasures. Notes Ekstrand, "The two artists . . . are credited with creating a whole new art of book illustration."[14]

Beyond Norway

Though the idea of trolls was born in Norway many centuries ago, they are no longer strictly a being of Norwegian imagination. Over the centuries trolls have become popular characters in the folktales of other parts of Scandinavia, including Iceland, Sweden, Finland, and Denmark. As is true with all folklore, the characteristics of trolls have undergone changes depending on who is telling the tale. For example, Icelandic troll tales feature a less social creature—one who would be unlikely to roam the forests with friends or siblings.

Swedish trolls also differ from those in the Norwegian stories. They are not nearly as ferocious or aggressive as their Norse relatives, nor do most of them differ much in appearance from humans, according to folklore expert John Lindow. "The trolls of Swedish popular belief were no larger than normal and generally of hideous appearance," he writes in *Swedish Legends and Folktales*. "They looked very much like the men and women one knew, the primary differentiating factors were that one did *not* know them, and that they were not Christians."[15]

The Swedish trolls sometimes do bad deeds but have never been considered inherently evil, as the Norse trolls are. "Swedish trolls are not quite as frightening," agrees Benson. "They are certainly more than capable of being mean occasionally, but are seen more as misunderstood. They are dim-witted and slow, that's for certain. They

can certainly be tricked by humans, but they definitely don't come across quite as monstrous in the Swedish stories."[16]

A Trollish Explanation

Whether they are seen as mischievous troublemakers or dangerous fiends, trolls have long provided Scandinavians with an explanation for trouble. "When things went wrong on the farm, there was a troll behind it," notes Benson. "The milk goes sour? It was a troll. If a farmer tripped in the field and hurt himself, the question was, Who put that stone there? It must have been a troll."[17]

Trolls have also provided a convenient excuse for forgetfulness or lapses in judgment. "If a fisherman was lost at sea, it was better to believe the sea troll had taken him than to admit he was foolish to have taken the boat out in such a storm," Ekstrand says. "If the farmer forgot to shut the gate at night, it was handy to blame the *nisse* [small farm troll] for turning the cow loose."[18]

In the twenty-first century, few people believe in the existence of trolls. Trolls are no longer an easy scapegoat for problems that befall humans. Even so, the stories of their run-ins with people and the trouble and confusion they cause are as entertaining today as they were many centuries ago.

Chapter 2

Bloodthirsty, Vicious, and Slow

There are many types of trolls, but the trolls that most commonly appear in folktales are of three types: mountain trolls, forest trolls, and sea trolls. All three are physically scary—both in appearance and demeanor. What makes them so frightening is their taste for human flesh—a preference that poses great risks for any unwary traveler who ventures too close.

The Largest Troll

Of all the trolls found in the stories of Scandinavia, the mountain troll is the largest and scariest. These trolls are often pictured with several heads, though some have just one. Although mountain trolls are said to have the strength of 50 strong humans, they are no match for the sun. It can turn them to stone in a fraction of a second. To avoid that fate, mountain trolls hide in caves during daylight hours. According to Florence Ekstrand, these trolls are portrayed in tales as spending their days "running thick grubby fingers through piles of gold, silver, and precious gems"[19] that have been mined by gnomes and elves who share the troll's mountain paradise.

The size of mountain trolls varies from story to story, but one of the most memorable descriptions of size appears in the story of Dyre Vaa, a young man from high in the mountains of Telemark, Norway, on the shores of Lake Totak. The story begins long ago, on a moonless Christmas Eve. Everyone in the town can hear a horrible, deep-throated yowling echoing from across the lake. According to one version of this story, the noise is "like a hundred oxen lowing nearby."[20] The night is exceedingly dark, but Vaa is not afraid; he steps into his boat and rows to the other side of the lake to investigate.

After reaching the far shore, he hears a loud yell, and though it is so dark that he can see nothing at all, Vaa knows by the booming voice that it belongs to a very tall troll. The troll is uncharacteristically civil because he needs a favor. He wants to visit several of his trollish lady friends, he explains, but they are far across the lake in Glomshill—even further away than Vaa's village. Since the lake is so deep, it is slow to freeze over. As a result, the troll says, he cannot walk, and so he needs someone to row him there. Vaa agrees to row the troll to Glomshill, but when the troll tries to get into the boat, they almost sink. "You must shrink a bit first," Vaa tells the troll. "My boat is so small and you are so tall. And it's dark."[21]

Did You Know?

In various troll tales, some of the fiercest and most conniving troll-wives are described as carrying their head under their armpit as they walk.

In an instant, Vaa can sense that the troll has used his magic to shrink himself, because the boat has become steadier. As he rows, Vaa tries to make conversation, asking the troll how big he actually is. The troll does not tell him. Instead, the troll promises to leave Vaa a token in the boat to show him just how big he actually is. When they arrive at Glomshill, the night is still very dark and Vaa is still unable to see the troll. However, Vaa hears him getting out of the boat, and afterward he begins the long journey back

home. At first light the next morning, Vaa runs down to his boat and finds evidence of the troll's immense size. The troll has left him just one finger of his glove—a finger so huge that it can hold four big baskets of wool.

The Wading Troll-Wife

Enormous size is not a characteristic of only male trolls. One story illustrates the amazing size of the females, too—usually referred to as "troll-hags" or "troll-wives." In this story a troll-wife decides to wade across the Norwegian Sea from Norway to Iceland. She knows that there are deep channels on the way but tells her neighbor, who is also a troll-wife, "Deep are Iceland's channels, but yet they can well be waded."[22] She does admit that there is one narrow, deep channel halfway across, so deep it will come to the top of her head, but she is certain that she will be able to step over it.

The troll-wife sets out, eventually coming to the deep channel. To help keep her balance, she tries to grab the top of a tall ship that is sailing past but misses the ship, falls into the channel, and drowns. According to a version of the tale collected by folklorist William A. Craigie, her body eventually washes ashore in Iceland, where people note that it is "so large that a man on horseback could not with his whip reach up to the bend of her knees, as she lay stiff and dead on the shore."[23]

The Forest Troll

Though not quite as big as the mountain troll, the forest troll is by far the uglier of the two. Like the mountain troll, this type of troll is sometimes portrayed with one head and other times with multiple heads. It can have as many as nine heads—each acting independently, arguing and screaming at one another. Forest trolls also are said to suffer from poor vision, as well as excruciating headaches. It is not unusual for some multiheaded forest trolls

A multiheaded mountain troll climbs toward its lair in this 1905 painting by Theodor Kittelsen.

Too Many Heads, Too Many Voices

In "The Dying Mountain Troll," a folktale written by Theodor Kittelsen, the central figure is a fierce, 12-headed mountain troll who is trying to figure out a way to add the gold of the sun to his stash of gems and precious metals. In one passage the story demonstrates not only the difficulty of thinking for any creature with that many heads, but also that the troll's ferocity can be multiplied by the number of heads it possesses.

> It's not so easy to think, either; that can be just as difficult as finding a sun. A twelve-headed troll finds it hard to reach an agreement with himself. There is no peace when all the heads must jaw at each other. Oh, yes, there was quite a ruckus on Ratamuten [mountain]! They spit and sputtered, made faces at each other and butted heads when the notion seized them. The only quiet thing was the body part on which they all sat. All night the squabbling continued. Fy! What nastiness! It sounded like the banging on iron plates, like rubbing stone on glass, like the drone of spinning wheels, like noisy grinding machines, caterwauling, flooding out over the night.

Quoted in Florence Ekstrand, *Norwegian Trolls and Other Tales.* Seattle: Welcome, 1990, pp. 109–10.

to kidnap humans (often beautiful princesses) to massage their heads—the only known cure for the pain of the headaches.

Forest trolls are known for possessing other unusual physical characteristics, as is illustrated in a tale of two young boys from a poor family walking in Norway's Hedale Woods. The boys are horrified when they hear the sound of trolls approaching. They know they are in real trouble when they hear one of the trolls declare, "I smell the smell of Christian blood here."[24]

When the voices come closer to the underbrush where they are hiding, the boys are astonished to see that what they first thought was a single three-headed troll turns out to be three forest trolls who share a single eye among them. According to Peter Asbjornsen and Jorgen Moe, the trolls are enormous, and they pass the eye from one to the other so that each troll might see what lies ahead: "[The trolls] were so big and tall that their heads were level with the tops of the fir trees. But they had only one eye among the three of them, and they took turns using it. Each had a hole in his forehead to put it in, and guided it with his hands. The one who went ahead had to have [the eye], and the others went behind him and held onto him."[25]

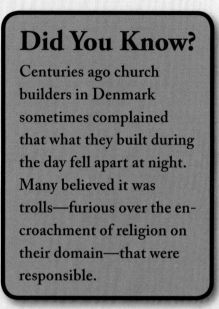

Did You Know?

Centuries ago church builders in Denmark sometimes complained that what they built during the day fell apart at night. Many believed it was trolls—furious over the encroachment of religion on their domain—that were responsible.

Quick Thinking

The boys know that though the trolls have vision problems, the troll sense of smell will surely lead them to the boys' hiding place. The older boy decides that it is best to deal with the situation bravely. He tells his brother to run ahead so that the trolls will chase him. The older boy sneaks behind the trolls pursuing his brother and, using his small hatchet, hits the last troll in the ankle. The troll screams in pain, and in the ensuing confusion, the troll in front drops the eye, which the older brother quickly scoops up.

Asbjornsen describes the eye as not only monstrously big, but also clear seeing on a dark night. "It was bigger than two quart pots put together," he writes, "and so clear and bright, that though it was pitch dark, everything was as clear as day as soon as he looked through it."[26]

The older brother, though not terribly strong, is both brave and smart. Using the eye as a bargaining chip, the boys agree to give it back to the trolls if they give the boys some special gifts—in this case, two beautiful crossbows for hunting and several sacks of gold. The trolls, who are unable to move without their eye, are forced to agree to the boys' terms, and the boys return home as heroes.

Sea Trolls

Like those who rule the forests and the mountains, the sea trolls of Scandinavia's folktales are gigantic. They are mean and unforgiving, and they have no use for humans other than for a meal. They live in the deepest parts of the ocean, but they surface occasionally to terrorize fishers and sailors and will kill and eat them if given a chance.

According to illustrator Theodor Kittelsen, a full-grown sea troll is said to have a mouth "as big as a haywagon."[27] Like mountain trolls, however, they can use magic to make themselves bigger or smaller, depending on the situation. At first glance, a sea troll looks very much like an enormous lobster. "He is in no way a crustacean," notes Ekstrand, "even though barnacles build little kingdoms on him as on a clam shell. He is swathed in trailing sea weeds and moss, his fingers are powerful, grasping."[28]

In one old tale, a fisher named Elias has an encounter with a sea troll. When Elias first begins throwing his line out, he has plenty of bites, but each time he brings up the line, there is no fish, nor is there any bait left on the hook. That seems odd to him, and after a time he becomes more frustrated. Searching in his knapsack, he finds an old

> **Did You Know?**
>
> Tales of river trolls make clear that they prefer rocky, fast-moving streams because these allow them better cover for hiding before attacking their human or animal prey.

green mitten and fills it with sand and filth that he scoops up from the bottom of the boat. He attaches it to his hook and lets the line out once more.

It does not take long until he feels a hard tug on the line—so hard it almost rips the line from his hands. Wrapping the line around the oarlock of the boat for support, he manages to pull it slowly toward the surface. Suddenly, an ugly sea troll rises out of the water with the green mitten hooked in its mouth. Angry and frightened, Elias rips the hook loose, spits in the troll's gaping mouth, and hurls the creature back into the sea.

Revenge of a Sea Troll

Many years later Elias rows to a deserted island to fish. During a break, he takes a walk to watch the seabirds and enjoy the unseasonably warm afternoon. As he walks back toward his boat, he notices what look like the dried-up remains of a sea otter on the sand.

He gives the creature a nudge with his foot and then gets the biggest shock of his life. What he had thought was a dead sea otter suddenly "leaped and barked and spurted water as if it were crazy,"[29] says Ekstrand. Elias kicks it as hard as he can, and when it rolls into the water, he realizes what it actually is. As the thing swells and swells, it takes on the shape of a large troll, with a nightmarish mouth that Ekstrand describes as "the size of an open coffin."[30]

Elias immediately recognizes the creature as the sea troll he encountered while fishing years before. The ugly creature taunts Elias, calling out, "Now you can spit in my mouth one more time if you wish, Elias!"[31] But Elias does not stay to listen. He rows his boat home as though his life depends on it—which it probably does.

"Three Billy Goats Gruff"

Though there are various types of trolls, most of them share one great weakness—they are slow-witted. This is why in many old tales, humans often outsmart the trolls. Outsmarting a troll is actually not that hard, which is why humans are not the only creatures who can get the best of a troll. In the classic tale "Three Billy Goats Gruff," three goats come out on top in a contest of wits with a troll. "That maybe says something about how intelligent a troll is, that three goats could outwit him!"[32] says folklorist Steve Benson.

The troll in this classic tale is a river troll that lives under a bridge. The story begins as spring arrives, and the three goats (who all share the last name of Gruff) decide to spend the day grazing in a mountain meadow. To get there the goats must cross a bridge with a troll living underneath. The troll in this story, Joanne Asala notes, "was fairly average as far as trolls go. He was big, and ugly, and hairy, with eyes as round as saucers and teeth as sharp as knives."[33]

The goats decide to make the journey despite the danger. They decide to cross the bridge one at a time. That way, maybe the troll will not even notice they are there. The first to go is the youngest, Jakkob Gruff. He begins to clop over the bridge, when all of a sudden the troll roars. When he sees the little goat, he tells the goat he will gobble him up. But Jakkob, in a tiny, scared voice, points out how small he is and how the troll would be much smarter to wait for his brother, who is a great deal fatter.

The troll agrees. Soon after, the second goat, Olaf Gruff, comes clopping over the bridge. Again, the troll announces that he is going to eat the goat, but Olaf quickly informs him that his big brother is right behind him and that he will make a much better meal. Again, the troll agrees to let the goat pass, anticipating the large, tasty meal that is to come.

Finally Ole Gruff, the third brother, begins crossing the bridge. As earlier, the troll announces that he plans to eat the goat, but Ole is not afraid. "Do your worst!" says Ole Gruff. "I've got two spears

A supremely ugly forest troll fights with a man in this Theodor Kittelsen illustration from 1890.

and I'll poke your eyes right out of your head!"[34] And that is exactly what happens. The goat charges and rams the troll, poking out both eyes and knocking him into the water. No one, according to the tale, was ever bothered again by the fierce troll—and the goats grew sleek and fat, gorging themselves on the sweet grass growing in the mountain pasture.

The Ash Lad

The three billy goats aside, in most of the old tales it is a human—often a young boy—who figures out a way to defeat the vicious troll. The boy is known as Askeladden, Norwegian for "the Ash Lad." He is usually the youngest boy in the family, a daydreamer, and appears far less strong, brave, or smart than his siblings. He is called Ash Lad because he spends a lot of his time in front of the hearth rooting around in the ashes while he daydreams. But while he may seem uninterested in the activity and conversations going on around him and may sometimes even seem simpleminded, the Ash Lad proves himself in the tales to be anything but that.

> **Did You Know?**
>
> "Three Billy Goats Gruff," which features a fierce river troll, is the most popular troll story with readers around the world.

"The Ash Lad Who Has an Eating Match with a Troll" is a good example of such a story. The story begins as an old farmer is worrying about the money he owes for his farm. He has a large forest on his property and decides that by cutting down some of the trees and selling the wood, he can pay off his debts. Being old and somewhat feeble, he realizes he must rely on his sons to do the cutting. The outlook is not terribly promising, however, for none of them seems competent to do such labor.

The oldest boy, complaining all the while, begins chopping at a tree when a large forest troll stumbles out of the darkest depths of the woods. "If you chop down the trees in my forest," he thunders,

Slower than Slow

Though bloodthirsty and powerful, trolls are usually portrayed in folktales as slow and dim-witted. One very old, very short troll story uses humor to show how extremely slow the troll's thought process is—especially when speaking with other trolls. It begins as a troll on one mountain thunders, "Does anyone hear that cow bellowing?"

Seven years later, a troll on a mountain nearby replies, "How do you know that isn't a bull and not a cow?

Another seven years goes by, and a seaweed-covered sea troll lifts his huge head out of the water and yells, "Will you two please shut up and stop shouting? I can't even hear myself think!"

Inez Knutsen, personal interview with the author, February 11, 2011, Bloomington, MN.

"I'll kill you."[35] Without replying, the frightened boy throws down his ax and runs home as fast as he can.

Disgusted with the cowardice of his oldest son, the farmer sends the middle son to do the chopping. But the same thing happens. Just as the boy begins to chop a scraggly pine tree, the troll lumbers out of the woods. He threatens to kill the boy, who quickly throws down his ax and runs for home. His father is as disgusted with him as with the oldest son.

The youngest boy, who is referred to as "Boots" or "The Ash Lad" in various versions of the story, is a dreamer. He volunteers to go, even though his brothers mock him mercilessly. "You!" they say. "Indeed! You'll do it bravely, no doubt—you, who've never been beyond the front door!"[36] But Boots ignores their teasing and asks his mother to pack him a large supply of food in his knapsack, especially a lot of cheese curds—his favorite snack. With a wave, Boots leaves on what seems like an impossible mission.

The Eating Contest

The troll is waiting at the forest's edge and threatens Boots just as he threatened his older brothers. Surprisingly, however, Boots fires right back. "Watch your tongue and mind your manners!" he yells. "Or I'll squeeze you like I'm squeezing the water out of this white stone!"[37] And with that, he reaches into his knapsack and grabs a large cheese curd and squeezes until water runs out of it. The troll has no idea that the stone is actually cheese; instead, he thinks he is seeing an exceptionally strong human. He instantly backs down and says that if Boots spares his life, he is free to take as many trees as he needs. Not only that, says the troll, but he will help Boots do the chopping. In no time at all, Boots has all the wood he needs.

At this point in the story, darkness has fallen, and the troll invites Boots to have a meal with him. Boots suggests to the troll that they have some fun by having an eating contest. The troll, thinking about how good it would taste to eat the boy, agrees. The troll takes out a gigantic black pot and begins to make a huge amount of oatmeal. Then the troll fills each of their bowls. While he is doing this, Boots empties his knapsack and slides it under his shirt, making sure the top is open.

Boots eats what he can, but then begins to sneak large spoonfuls into the open top of his knapsack. When the sack is full, he takes out his knife and rips a hole in it so that the uneaten oatmeal can pour out. The troll, busily eating, does not notice and is surprised that Boots seems to be keeping up with him in the contest. Boots comments that he is not even half full. Impressed, the troll asks Boots how he is able to eat so much. Boots replies, "Easy. Do as I did. You take your knife and make a hole in your stomach, then you can eat as much as you wish!"[38]

The troll is astonished, and he asks Boots if it hurts. "Oh, nothing to speak of,"[39] Boots shrugs. And with that assurance, the troll stabs himself with his knife—and that is the end of him. Boots then grabs the troll's silver and gold and heads for home.

His father and brothers are astonished at Boots's success. Between the troll's treasure and the chopped wood, the farmer is able to pay off his debt.

The trolls that appear in these and scores of other tales have a fierce and frightening disposition. But in these stories humans almost always find ways to vanquish the slow-witted trolls. They do not overpower them physically, for that would be virtually impossible. As the stories make clear, humans who rely on courage and cunning will always triumph over trolls.

Chapter 3

The Troll Family Tree

Though most trolls portrayed in folktales are fierce monsters that are life threatening to humans who come into contact with them, they are not all that way. Folklorists say that the troll family tree is wide ranging. It encompasses a number of strange creatures, some of which do not kill or eat people. A few might even be helpful to humans on occasion, though they, too, are more than capable of causing trouble and heartache for any humans they meet. In many cases those who treat these troll-relatives poorly can expect to be treated in kind. After all, folklorists say, these creatures *are* still part of the troll family tree.

The Hulder-Folk

Among the close relatives of trolls are the hulder-folk. In the old tales, the hulder-folk are hidden—some underground, others in out-of-the-way places where no human can see them. The term *hulder* comes from a Norwegian word meaning "covered." Hulder-folk live in an environment of perpetual twilight, where they herd their cattle, raise their children, and live their long lives.

The reason the hulder-folk are hidden is explained in a legend that is a mixture of ancient Norse folklore and the biblical story of the Creation. According to that legend, Eve is washing all of her many children when God arrives. Startled because some of her children have not yet been washed, and embarrassed that they are dirty, she hides them.

When God looks at the freshly scrubbed children, he praises Eve because her children are so beautiful. When God asks her if all her children are there, she lies and tells him yes, because she does not want him to be angry that she has not bathed them all. But God knows she is lying, and he tells her that those children she has hidden will remain hidden forever. At that exact moment, the children Eve hid vanish in nooks and crannies and under the nearby hills. Their descendants become the hulder-folk, or the hidden people—sometimes underground or hidden in the high hills or caves, where humans see them only when the hulder-folk wish to be seen.

The Beautiful Huldra

The hulder-folk are not as ugly as trolls, nor are they unnaturally large. Though folklorists say that they lack souls (just as trolls do), on the outside they look very much like humans—except that they have cow tails. The hulder-females (known as huldra) are very beautiful, although they, too, have cow tails.

Stories that revolve around a huldra resemble stories of mermaids. The huldra may try to get a young man to fall in love with her. The moment he does, she takes him down to her underground world, and once there, he can never return. Sometimes she accomplishes this in the same way mermaids attract sailors—by singing in a voice that is both haunting and beautiful.

Did You Know?

According to some stories a huldra has a life span of between 300 and 400 years.

In some stories, a young man who is searching for his lost cow hears the huldra's love song carried on the wind. As he follows the sound, notes Florence Ekstrand, he hears "a song so unutterably beautiful that tears stung at his eyes."[40] Even if the man is already married or engaged, he cannot resist; he will follow the huldra to her home. Within a few weeks, he will have completely forgotten his girlfriend or wife, his home, or any part of his life before he met the huldra.

A young boy seems more curious than scared by his encounter with a massive troll in "The Troll and the Boy" by artist John Bauer. Though most stories portray trolls as nasty troublemakers, some members of the troll family tree can actually be kind— when they want to be.

Sometimes Kind, Too

While huldra are often dangerous, they are portrayed in some stories as kind and generous to people who help them. The nineteenth-century folklorist Andreas Faye tells one story in which a huldra's true identity is kept secret by an act of human kindness. A huldra has happened upon a large human celebration, and she is excited to take part. Because she is breathtakingly attractive, she is soon the center of attention, as Faye writes:

> Everyone wanted to dance with the beautiful young girl. But while she was dancing with one of the men, he caught sight of her long tail. He realized at once what sort of creature he was dancing with, but he calmed his fears and said to her, "Fair maiden, you are losing your garter." She ran outdoors at once but later rewarded the considerate and discreet young lad with gifts of fine clothes and good cattle.[41]

In another legend, a poor peasant is out in the forest looking after his cattle when he finds a very young lamb lying by itself under a bush. Worried that the lamb is in danger of being killed by a wolf or other wild animal, the peasant wraps it in his shirt and carries it home to his wife. She pets the lamb and puts it on a blanket next to the stove in their cottage.

The following day the peasant goes back to the forest and hears a sad voice crying, "My child! My child! Where is my child?"[42] He looks around but can see no one. Confused and upset, he goes home and talks to his wife about the voice he had heard. The peasant and his wife are thunderstruck when the lamb dozing by the stove awakens and happily begins to talk to them, explaining that the voice is that of his mother. With that, the lamb scampers out the door and runs across the yard and into the deep forest.

The peasant and his wife know then that the lamb is actually the child of a huldra whose mother has shape-shifted her into the body of a lamb so the humans will not be frightened. Because the humans were so gentle with her child, the huldra repays them by giving the couple good luck with their cattle. From that day forward their cattle are the sleekest and healthiest of all the cattle in the land.

The Spirits of the Water

The shape-shifting ability of the huldra and her children is not unique in Scandinavian folktales. On one branch of the troll family tree is a group of shape-shifting male water spirits related to water trolls. The most dangerous of these are known as *nokken*, a Norse word meaning "water horse."

It is an appropriate name, because *nokken* often appear to humans disguised as a beautiful horse. When a human gets on the horse's back, however, the *nokken* jumps into the pond or river, taking the astonished rider with him. The rider is never seen again and is presumed to be either drowned or residing in the *nokken*'s underwater kingdom.

However, the *nokken* is not all-powerful. Just as trolls are both frightened and repulsed by the sound of church bells, the *nokken* is said to be terrified of anything made of steel. Many tales feature humans smart enough to carry a needle or other small tool made of steel, just in case they are tricked by a shape-shifting *nokken*.

> ### Did You Know?
>
> The fosse-grim, another member of the troll family found in Scandinavian folktales, lives within waterfalls and plays the violin so beautifully that no one can resist stopping to listen.

A Smart Farm Maid

One popular tale takes place on a lakeside farm in southern Sweden, where a young woman and her horse are plowing a field. It is a beautiful spring day—the kind that all Scandinavians appreciate after a long, snowy winter. The farm maid is enjoying the smell of the grass, the sound of insects, and the companionship of her plow horse, when an amazing thing happens.

The Huldra Loses Her Tail

There are some stories in which a huldra falls so deeply in love with a human man that she is willing to be married and remain aboveground with him. Before the wedding ceremony, she carefully conceals her cow tail beneath her beautiful wedding gown. However, the moment the pastor pronounces the wedding holy in the eyes of God, her tail magically falls off, and she becomes like any other human woman, only more beautiful.

According to the folktales, huldras make wonderful wives. They are wise and kind, and they are very skilled storytellers. Children born from such a marriage are usually exceptional, too. They often have the gift of second sight—the ability to see or dream things before they actually happen.

A horse suddenly appears out of the lake—big and beautiful, brown with large, white spots. The horse has a silver mane that flutters in the wind and a silky tail that reaches almost to the ground. As the girl stands admiring the animal, he prances up next to her and waits as if to encourage her to climb on his back. But the girl quickly realizes that the horse is likely a *nokken* and ignores him. Then the horse comes closer and closer, and finally he is so close that he could bite the plow horse. But the girl hits the strange horse with the bridle and screams at him, saying that if he does not disappear at once, she will make him plow the field.

The moment she says this, the *nokken* magically changes places with the plow horse and begins to plow the field. Unlike the real horse, however, the *nokken* does the work with such blinding speed that the astonished girl can barely hold on to the plow. In the time it takes a rooster to crow seven times, the plowing is finished, and the *nokken* begins running back toward the lake, dragging both the plow and the girl.

But the girl is prepared for just such an emergency—she has a little piece of steel in her pocket. The moment she grabs onto it and takes it from her pocket, the *nokken* disappears into the lake, taking the plow with him but leaving the girl behind. To this day people who visit or live near the lake say they can hear a frustrated neighing echoing from the lake's depths and see the deep track of the plow leading to the water.

The Changelings

Another creature whose appearance was once much feared by people was the changeling, a troll-child left by trolls who steal a human baby and then leave the changeling in its place. Stories offer several reasons why a troll would want to steal a human child. Sometimes it might be because a troll is angry with certain humans and wants to punish them by stealing their child. In other cases a troll-wife might be disappointed that her own child is ugly or sickly. Sometimes trolls are anxious to introduce a new strain of blood into the troll race or steal a human child to raise and train to be a servant.

Changelings appear in the folktales of Scandinavia as well as countries such as Germany, England, Wales, Ireland, and Spain. The tales are based on real fears of trolls or other magical beings who were thought to have the power to steal human babies and substitute their own children. Such fears were not uncommon prior to the Middle Ages and continued well into the seventeenth century. In some of the tales it is not readily apparent to the human parents that a changeling has been substituted for their baby. Perhaps the troll has used magic to make the troll-baby look human—at least for a while. Parents may think they detect a little difference in the cry of the in-

> ### Did You Know?
> The mysterious little tangles on a horse's tail are known as nisse-plaits—after the *nisse*, who sometimes braids the mane or tail of his favorite horse. In Scandinavian countries it is considered very bad luck to undo them.

fant or in the shape of the eyes, but nothing so dramatic that it would signal evidence of a changeling. Occasionally in folktales, more than a year or two goes by before the parents realize they have been caring for a child who is not their own.

In other cases the changeling is easy to identify. Peter Asbjornsen recounts an old tale about a woman who lived in Lesja, Norway, and received a changeling. In the tale the woman's descendant recalls the odd features of the changeling:

> I, of course, never saw him, for she was dead and he was gone long before I was ever born. But my father told me about him. He had the leathery face of an old man, but had eyes as red as a carp's, and they glowed in the dark like an owl's. His head was as long and thin as a horse's, and as big and round as a cabbage. He had legs as hairy as a sheep's and a body as bony as a starved chicken's.[43]

Guarding Against Changelings

The threat of a baby being stolen and replaced with a changeling was a constant fear for those who lived before and during the Middle Ages. Many a new mother was certain that the trolls were secretly spying on her and her newborn, waiting until the time was right to make the switch. Because of this fear, parents in folktales would take certain precautions, as Joanne Asala explains:

> The christening of a baby would protect it, and so babies were brought to the church as quickly as possible after birth. The child was never left alone; at night a candle was kept burning and a watch was set. The baby was never taken outside until the day of the christening and even then was protected by something made of steel—a pin or a knife. There were other charms as well—a prayer-book ... [or] a cross.[44]

According to the tales and accounts of changelings, it did not take long for trolls to switch their child for the human child. Sometimes it happened when the new mother nodded off to sleep. Even though she planned to be vigilant throughout the night, she was often simply too exhausted to keep her eyes open. Ekstrand tells a story from the 1840s of a Swedish woman who is absolutely convinced she had a very close call shortly after giving birth—even though she never actually sees the troll.

Her husband is helping with the grain harvest one evening, and she is alone with her newborn son, when suddenly she hears a sharp rap at the door. Ekstrand writes:

> Though she had locked the door from the inside, she had a chilling sense of someone else in the room with her. She jumped from the bed, grabbed a handful of straw from the mattress and threw it on the coals. As the flames lit the room there was another sharp rap. The room was empty except for her and the child. She believed it was a troll come to steal her baby boy and leave one of its own in his place.[45]

How to Deal with a Troll-Child

In many troll tales human parents are unsure of how to deal with a changeling. They may be uncertain even about whether the child is actually a troll-child, for the signs may not be conclusive. In one tale, for example, parents are horrified by the behavior of their child, now a toddler. He seems to spend most of his time whining and screaming, and whenever he gets hold of something, he throws it straight at his mother's head.

Conventional wisdom many centuries ago suggested that it was best to beat a changeling, for then the troll-mother would come to the child's rescue and switch the children back. But in this story the mother cannot bear the thought of beating her child. She refuses—even though the beating might bring back her own child. Days and

weeks go by, and things do not improve. But one day, just as the woman is sure she will die of a broken heart thinking of her lost child, she is astonished to see a little curly headed blond boy running toward her cottage. She knows by his look he must be her son, and when she sees a troll-mother lumbering behind him, she is certain.

The troll-mother tells her that because she has been kind to the changeling—never beating him even though she was advised to do so—she is returning her real child. Without another word, she grabs her troll-child and stomps off into the forest.

The Guardian of the Farm

Though folklorists say there are a large number of creatures on the troll family tree, they agree that the one least like the large, blood-thirsty trolls of the forests, seas, and mountains is known in Norway as the *nisse*, or in Sweden as a *tomte*. "Physically, he couldn't be more different from his troll brothers," says Inez Knutsen, "but that's only part of it. While we always learned in the stories that trolls try to avoid humans most of the time, the *nisse* lives in close proximity to people. He's smart, too—which is another difference between the *nisse* and a troll."[46]

He is indeed quite the op-posite of the large, hulking trolls. He is always portrayed as a tiny old man—ranging from less than 12 inches (30cm) high to the size of a toddler. In illustrations he appears as a tiny bearded man with a small, red, pointed cap. Like the *nokken*, the *nisse* has fiery, golden eyes that glow in the dark. He also has a tail, as do his troll-relatives. And although he is mostly a helpful creature, when crossed or treat-ed unfairly, he is quick to exact revenge.

The *nisse* has neither wife nor children, but chooses to live alone among the animals in the barn. He is the guardian of the farm and has been seen as that since the first settlers began establishing farms in Scandinavia—long before the coming of Christianity. From the

> ### Did You Know?
> Though the *nisse* is small, in some tales he is able to outrun a galloping horse.

No Butter on the Christmas Porridge

No story more vividly illustrates the volatile nature of the *nisse* than the one about a cook's helper who decides to play a little trick on the *nisse* by putting the butter on the bottom of his Christmas porridge instead of on the top. She hides behind a door to get a look at his face when he sees there is no butter but is horrified at what she actually sees.

The moment the *nisse* begins to eat and realizes that there is no butter on top, he flies into a rage. He runs into the stall of a brown cow that he lovingly tended all year and kills it. Still angry, he sits down and finishes his pudding—and sees the butter at the bottom of the bowl. Realizing his horrible mistake, the *nisse* wails and cries over what he has done. Later that night, he runs to another farm, carries off their best cow, and brings it home—even though the cow is not nearly as beautiful as the one he killed.

twelfth century on, church officials tried mightily (without much success) to outlaw belief in the *nisse*, because he represented the ancient pagan beliefs just as the ancient Norse gods and trolls did.

Strong and Strange

The *nisse* is complex, for to think of him merely as a tiny, kindly being who helps on the farm would be wrong. First, his size belies his amazing strength. Folklorist William A. Craigie tells the story of a young man who is dating a girl from a nearby farm. As he is walking her home one evening, he is amazed at what he sees. Craigie writes: "[They] saw a huge load of grain coming down the road; it was bigger than the biggest load of hay, yet there was no horse to it, but the *nisse* was under it, and carried the lot. When this arrived at the farm, the young fellow and the girl both saw the entrance lift itself up, so that the load could get in, and then come down into its place again."[47]

Craigie also tells a folktale about a peasant who meets a *nisse* on a road one winter evening and is very rude to him. The man orders the *nisse* to get out of the way. The *nisse*, who has very little patience for humans in the best of circumstances, reacts very quickly, throwing the peasant over the fence into a snowbank before the man even knows what is happening.

Loyalty to the Farm

The *nisse*'s loyalty is not to the farmer, nor even strictly to the animals—though he always seems to prefer the latter. Instead, he is always tied to the land itself. In fact, some folklore experts believe that the idea of the *nisse* may have originated from a superstition from ancient times, when the very first humans arrived in the North to farm. In parts of Scandinavia people once believed that the original owner of a plot of land, the farmer who first chopped down trees and tilled the soil, would continue to own the farm after he died. "In some parts of the country . . . [the original farmer] gradually developed into the *nisse*, who stayed with the farm generation after generation," notes Ekstrand, "seeing to it that the animals weren't mistreated but [at the same time] wreaking a certain discomfort on the folk of the farm."[48]

For example, the *nisse* takes great pains in making sure the livestock are well-fed and their stalls kept clean and dry. In the tales many a farmer walks into his barn and notices that the horses' coats are shinier than usual and their manes and tails have been combed and braided. The *nisse* may even have added to the feed supply by raiding a neighbor's farm and bringing home sacks of food for his favorite animals. On the other hand, as willing as the *nisse* is to help on the farm, he is definitely not someone a farmer should take for granted.

The Vindictive Nisse

The *nisse* asks for very little in return for his hard work. He is content with a dish of porridge on Christmas Eve. But if he does not receive his porridge, or if he is mistreated or slighted in any other way, he can be very vindictive. In one old tale a certain *nisse* gets along very well with the farmer but does not care at all for the farmer's wife. One day when the farmer has gone to town, the wife demands that the *nisse* use his magic to provide each of her sons with the equivalent of $1,000. If he does not, she warns, she will pick the *nisse* up and throw him into the fire. He first refuses but finally does as she asks, and the woman happily gathers the money, puts it in a bag, and buries it in the garden.

A little while later the farmer returns and sees the *nisse* looking sad and upset. He asks whether the *nisse* would like to come out to the stable and have a drop from the keg, but the *nisse* refuses. He tells the farmer that he is leaving and explains what the farmer's wife has done. "You have been kind to me," he says, "and I will say farewell and thanks to you. Here are some little stones for you, which I will give you as a parting-gift."[49]

> # Did You Know?
> The bite of the *nisse*, according to some tales, is so poisonous that people are likely to shrivel and die before a doctor can reach them.

Soon after the *nisse* leaves, things begin to go wrong. The animals become sick and bony, and the land becomes overrun with weeds. The farmer's sons die, one after another, and the money runs out. Soon after all this happens, the farmer's wife sneaks out to the garden and digs up the bag of money. When she opens the bag, however, she is horrified to see that the money has turned to stones. "At this," says Craigie, "[the farmer's wife] was so angry and vexed, that she fell down dead on the spot."[50]

Now alone, the farmer decides one day to have a look at the little stones his *nisse* gave him. When he opens the drawer, he is astonished to see that the stones have somehow turned into gold coins. "'Vengeful' is the word that comes to mind whenever I read that story," says Knutsen. "You can read some [tales] and almost forget the *nisse* has that malicious side to him. He can be kind and delightful, but in certain stories the *nisse*'s trollish nature is pretty evident. People who treat him badly always find that by doing so, they are putting themselves at very great risk."[51]

That any of the members of the troll family tree are totally capable of causing trouble occasionally should not startle anyone. "My grandfather always said, 'You know, you shouldn't ever be surprised—a troll is a troll,'" says Knutsen. "I guess it's just a matter of degrees."[52]

Chapter 4

Beyond the Early Legends

Because trolls are such unusual and dislikable characters, it is hardly surprising that folktales about them have survived. But trolls and their relatives are not limited to old stories from Norway and other parts of Scandinavia. Trolls continue to intrigue writers and storytellers from all over the world. And while they may differ in some ways from the trolls of old, many of these more contemporary trolls have retained the savage ferocity for which the trolls of folklore are best known.

Peer Gynt and the Trolls

One of the most famous literary uses of trolls is in *Peer Gynt*, a five-act play by Norwegian dramatist Henrik Ibsen that premiered in February 1876. Written entirely in verse, the play tells the story of a young man, Peer Gynt, who seems to be wasting his life by avoiding responsibility and hard work. At the beginning of the play, the audience sees Peer lying about his accomplishments, much to the scorn of others around him.

In the first act, Peer flirts with a young woman, and when she is reluctant to dance with him, he teases her by pretending to be a troll: "I can turn myself into a troll!" he growls:

> ## Did You Know?
>
> In the award-winning movie trilogy *Lord of the Rings*, the trolls are portrayed as having very short noses and black blood.

At midnight I'll come and stand by your bed.
If you hear something hissing and spitting
Don't comfort yourself it's only a cat.
It will be me! I'll drain out your blood
Into a cup, and as for your little sister—
I'll gobble her up. . . .[53]

In one scene of the play, Peer has a bad hangover from drinking at a wedding the previous evening and knocks himself unconscious after he runs into a rock. While unconscious, he dreams that he meets a young woman dressed entirely in green who says she is the daughter of the King of the Trolls. She agrees to take Peer to the mountain where her father sits on a throne, a scepter in his hand. There the young trolls and goblins and even a huldra dance around Peer, begging permission from the king to rip him limb from limb. In Peter Asbjornsen's translation of the play, the dialogue demonstrates the trolls' violent nature:

> Trolls: Kill him! Kill the scoundrel who has dared to tempt the king's fair daughter!
> Troll Child: Let me chop off his fingers!
> Second Troll Child: Let me at him! I'll rip his hair out!
> Huldra Maiden: I'll bite him until he's black and blue!
> Trollkjerring [troll-witch]: I'll boil him down for our soup tonight!
> A second Trollkjerring: Toasted on a spit, or boiled in a kettle, which shall it be?[54]

Making Choices

The Troll King says that if Peer becomes a troll, he will have permission to marry his daughter, the woman in green. He asks Peer what he believes to be the difference between humans and trolls, and Peer

Theodor Kittelsen's "Forest Troll" illustration, published in 1906, presents a wholly disagreeable but also enduringly intriguing character.

answers that he sees no difference. If people were more courageous to act the way they really feel, he says, they would be far more troll-like. Says Peer to the Troll King:

No difference [between humans and trolls] at all, it seems to me.
Big trolls roast you, little trolls scratch you;
It's the same with us, when we're brave enough.[55]

In the end, Peer decides that he does not really want to become a troll, and he escapes from the mountain. And while Peer's interaction with the trolls is just one part of *Peer Gynt*, those scenes have resonated with playgoers for many years.

According to writer Julie Jensen McDonald, the story of Peer Gynt and his adventures makes readers think hard about their own lives and the choices they make. Ibsen makes the point that people spend much of their lives learning to control selfishness, anger, cruelty, and other trollish impulses. "How many of us are living as trolls and keeping it a secret?"[56] McDonald asks.

The Music of Trolls

For many who attended the play, the experience of seeing *Peer Gynt* was made even more enjoyable because of the musical score by Norwegian composer Edvard Grieg. In 1874 Ibsen approached the 24-year-old Grieg and asked him to compose some incidental music for *Peer Gynt*. Of the 90 minutes of music Grieg composed, it was one particular piece that captivated playgoers more than any other. It was named, appropriately, "In the Hall of the Mountain King."

The piece begins after Peer hits his head. In a dream he meets the Mountain King's daughter, who invites him to visit the royal hall. The music is at first tentative and soft as Peer Gynt nervously creeps into the room, but the score gets louder and faster as the gob-

A Modern Look at Changelings

Some folklorists believe that the idea of changelings may be a very early explanation for babies born with physical or mental disabilities. Notes troll expert Joanne Asala:

> The belief in changelings probably arose from the desire of parents to have healthy, normal children. Today, parents usually accept the fact when their child has a physical or mental [disability], but our ancestors did not. Handicapped and critically ill children were often not accepted by their parents and were either abused or neglected. Some parents believed that their own child had been kidnapped by trolls and replaced with a baby not their own—a troll changeling.

Joanne Asala, *Norwegian Troll Tales*. Iowa City, IA: Penfield, 2005, p. 128.

lins and trolls discover him and taunt him. The end is dramatic, with the crashing of cymbals and the deafening roar as the trolls dance around the king's throne.

Though audiences loved the music, Grieg was unsure of its value at the time—convinced that the piece was too heavy-handed. Frequently overcritical of his own work, he confided to a friend that it was "something I literally can't stand to listen to because it absolutely reeks of cow-pies, ultra-Norwegian-ness and trollish self-sufficiency."[57]

Music lovers disagree, however. They praise the piece's eerie minor key and bouncy, lurching notes that seem just right for the way trolls move. "In the Hall of the Mountain King" has become one of the most recognizable, exciting pieces in the history of classical music. Not only is it performed by symphony orchestras around the world, it has been recorded by a range of modern musical groups from the Who to the Trans Siberian Orchestra. The song was even used once as a melody whistled by a serial killer in the scary 1931 movie *M*.

Trolls in Middle Earth

Trolls also play a part in J.R.R. Tolkien's fantasy novels *The Hobbit* and *The Lord of the Rings*. Tolkien's trolls share many characteristics with the trolls of the old folktales, such as their enormous size and strength, their stupidity, and their tendency to turn to stone when subjected to the sun's rays.

Bilbo Baggins, the hero of *The Hobbit,* is a hobbit—a small creature related to humans. Early in the story Baggins and some companions meet three stone trolls (so named because of their vulnerability to sunlight) whose favorite foods are mutton, hobbits, and dwarves. The trolls' names are William, Bert, and Tom, and the three are sitting in the woods eating beside a fire. Though he has never actually seen one before, Baggins knows at once they are trolls. Writes Tolkien, "Even Bilbo, in spite of his sheltered life, could see that: from the great heavy faces of them, and their size, and the shape of their legs, not to mention their language, which was not drawing-room fashion at all, at all."[58]

If he has any doubt about their identity at all, it vanishes as he hears the one named Tom complain that the journey, which was William's idea, has been hard because of the lack of food (especially humans):

> Never a blinking bit of manflesh have we had for long enough. . . . "What the 'ell William was a-thinking of to bring us into these parts at all, beats me—and the drink runnin' short, what's more," he said jogging the elbow of William, who was taking a pull at his jug.

William choked. "Shut yer mouth!" he said as soon as he could. "Yer can't expect folk to stop here for ever just to be et by you and Bert. You've et a village and a half between yer, since we come down from the mountains. How much more d'yer want?"[59]

As in classic Scandinavian tales, Bilbo and his friends are able to escape the trolls by outwitting them. They disguise their voices to sound like the trolls themselves and confound the creatures. William, Bert, and Tom are so absorbed in the confusing conversation they do not notice that the sun is coming up. In a single instant as the sun rises over the horizon, the three trolls turn to stone. "And there they stand to this day," writes Tolkien, "all alone, unless the birds perch on them; for trolls, as you probably know, must be underground before dawn, or they go back to the stuff of the mountains they are made of, and never move again."[60]

Trolls in Harry Potter's World

Trolls appear as characters in more modern literature, too. For example, they are mentioned several times in J.K. Rowling's Harry Potter series. In the first book, *Harry Potter and the Sorcerer's Stone*, Harry and his best friends, Ron and Hermione, fight a battle with a dangerous mountain troll that has invaded Hogwarts School of Witchcraft and Wizardry. When Harry and Ron hear a frantic announcement that a troll has been spotted inside Hogwarts, they know that they must warn their friend Hermione, who has not heard the announcement because she is in the bathroom.

> **Did You Know?**
>
> When disagreeable teacher Dolores Umbridge confiscates Harry Potter's Quidditch broom in *Harry Potter and the Order of the Phoenix,* she orders trolls to guard it.

To their horror, however, they find that the troll is in the bathroom, too, and has already spotted Hermione. According to Rowling's story, Ron and Harry know the troll is there even before they see him. "Harry sniffed," she writes, "and a foul stench reached his nostrils, a mixture of old socks and the kind of public toilet no one ever seems to clean."[61]

When the troll comes into view, its appearance is as disgusting as its smell. Rowling writes: "It was a horrible sight. Twelve feet tall, its skin was a dull, granite gray, its great lumpy body like a boulder with its small bald head perched on top like a coconut. It had short legs thick as tree trunks with flat, horny feet. The smell coming from it was incredible. It was holding a huge wooden club, which dragged along the floor because its arms were so long."[62]

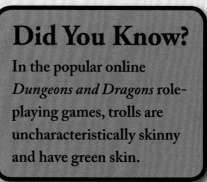

Did You Know?

In the popular online *Dungeons and Dragons* role-playing games, trolls are uncharacteristically skinny and have green skin.

As in classic troll tales, the three friends are able to subdue the troll by working together. Harry leaps onto the troll's back, and his wand becomes lodged in the troll's nose. Howling with pain, the troll swings its club, which flies out of its hand. Ron, who has had a great deal of difficulty in class with magic spells, yells the first one that comes into his mind. Immediately, the club lands with a thud on the troll's head, knocking it unconscious.

Trolls Online

Another type of troll exists in the twenty-first century. The word *troll* has been used to identify a person who posts on an Internet website, hoping to disrupt the conversation on a blog or discussion forum. Instead of writing a comment related to the topic at hand, the troll writes something that will inflame others, cause anger or confusion, or just destroy the online dialogue. It is not difficult to see what this modern-day troll has in common with the trolls of folklore—he or she is a verbal bully.

Sometimes these trolls are merely annoying to those serious posters who are interested in having an online conversation about a particular topic. "It's like the online version of some fool in a bar walking over to a perfect stranger and deciding to pick a fistfight," says Jerry Shapiro, a Chicago Bears fan who enjoys participating on the team's message boards after a game. Shapiro adds:

> I don't think there's anyone who doesn't find trolls annoying, except other trolls. You can be . . . just having a conversation about what might have gone wrong, or why [Bears' coach] Lovie Smith decided on running that particular play like settling for kicking a field goal instead of going for the touchdown. Whatever, it's just what a lot of fans do, you know? And then you have some guy who decides to take the conversation in a whole different direction, like saying, "The Bears lost because the coach is black," or something really stupid like that. I mean, it's totally ridiculous. The troll is just hoping someone takes the bait and gets mad and starts arguing with him.[63]

The Cruelty of Trolls

Some online trolls are more than simply annoying. Their posts can be hurtful and cruel, too. In March 2011, a California 13-year-old named Rebecca Black posted her own music video on YouTube. The video of the song "Friday" was professional-quality—a gift from her mother, who said her daughter's dream was to become a professional singer someday. "I thought it would be a good experience and would give her a glimpse of what it takes,"[64] her mother said in an interview.

Rebecca says that while many who viewed the video were supportive and complimentary, she was unprepared for some of the trolling she received. Some not only left comments critical of her singing, but also about her physical appearance. "Those hurtful comments really shocked me," she told one reporter. "At times, it feels like I'm being cyberbullied."[65]

Trolls and Artemis Fowl

Trolls also play a part in the popular Artemis Fowl fantasy series by Eoin Colfer. In these books, trolls are considered the most deadly members of the fairy race. Like the legendary trolls, Colfer's trolls are nervous about being exposed to light; however, instead of being turned to stone by light, these trolls are driven insane by it. They are also very sensitive to both water and loud noises. They do have a weapon not possessed by Scandinavian trolls: curved, sharp tusks with serrated edges—perfect for gutting any prey they might encounter. Some trolls have tusks with a strong sedative that could quickly disarm even the strongest human who tried to resist.

The Gentling of the Trolls

As many modern trolls in literature and on the Internet have retained (and have even surpassed) the cruelty of those trolls in the old folktales, some modern-day versions of Scandinavia's traditional trolls have become tamer. Folklorists say that troll stories and images have mellowed over time. Artists, woodcutters, and storytellers in the twenty-first century are more likely to show a troll as a bumbling, silly prankster than a ferocious creature eager to consume as many humans as possible.

The reinvention of the troll's mean and nasty reputation began in the twentieth century as a flood of immigrants from Scandinavian countries poured into the United States, especially in the years after World War II. Though many of these immigrants brought the old folktales with them, many felt that the troll tales were too scary for children. Over the years the troll's rough edges were smoothed, and trolls were no longer presented as the frightening creatures they once were. From woodcarvings and children's picture books to Saturday morning cartoons, trolls have become more elflike than monstrous.

Troll Dolls

Of all the ways the troll's image was made gentler, none was as effective as a diminutive doll made by a Danish woodcarver named Thomas Dam in 1959. Dam did not have much money to buy his daughter a Christmas gift that year, so he decided to carve a little troll doll, which delighted her. When her friends saw the little troll, they all wanted one, too, so Dam created his own company called DAM Things and began selling dolls (made of hard rubber rather than carved wood) throughout Denmark.

The popularity of these dolls, with their glass eyes and long wool hair, spread quickly. However, because of a mistake in the copyright paperwork, a number of other manufacturers were able to use Dam's doll as a model to make their own, cheaper versions of troll dolls. Soon the little dolls flooded toy stores throughout Europe and the United States.

Though just a few inches tall, the troll doll is easy to spot with its signature wild hair—usually of a vivid color such as lavender, orange, or fluorescent green. Trolls dolls have odd, smiley faces, and while no one would ever call one pretty, many troll doll fans think they are winsome. The troll dolls have spawned T-shirts, gummy candy, and even television cartoons based on their adventures. They remain popular in the twenty-first century, not only with children but with adult collectors as well.

The Value of Trolls

Not everyone agrees that a gentler sort of troll is an appropriate change for a creature with such a long history of being mean. "They are too cute for me today," Inez Knutsen complains. She explains:

> The troll is neither an elf, nor a funny little guy with long pink hair. My granddaughter has several of those [dolls]. She

loves them, and that's fine. But I say to her, "Trolls are everything that is bad, everything that is crude and mean. That's their nature, to be that way. So fine—get these cute little dolls with their smiling faces and colorful hair. But let's call them something else, for they are definitely not trolls."[66]

Author Lise Lunge-Larsen is also a staunch advocate of preserving the old troll tales. She believes that while the troll tales of old may be frightening, they have always played a valuable role in the lives of children. "Everything about the troll is contradictory to human nature," she writes. She explains:

> They are enormous, grotesque creatures with superhuman strength. They are full of treachery and falseness and stand for all that is base and evil. To fight trolls, you can't be like them or use their weapons. Thus battling trolls brings out the very best in those who dare confront them: intelligence and ingenuity, courage and persistence, kindness and pluck, and the ability of men and women to rely on what each has to offer.[67]

The best lesson of troll tales is simple: for a human to prevail over brutish trolls is to rely on the best aspects of his or her humanity—the things that make humans different from trolls. It might be kindness, loyalty, or imagination—or a combination of such traits—that helps a person defeat a troll.

"It's not even just the old troll folktales; I believe that's true even with modern literature that includes trolls," says Lunge-Larsen. "When you read in *Harry Potter* how the three friends overcome the troll by working together—that's the complete opposite of how trolls operate. They are helping one another, being kind, being loyal, and that goes against everything that trolls stand for. They are fighting against the troll for all the right reasons. That's a key lesson that those [troll] tales can teach."[68]

Though most troll tales are set in a time many centuries past, these stories still resonate with readers and listeners of all ages. The very idea of such cruel, brutal beings is frightening but the knowledge that trolls *can* be defeated also appeals to people as much today as to those who heard the same stories so long ago.

Source Notes

Introduction: Trolls on the Prowl

1. Inez Knutsen, personal interview with the author, February 11, 2011, Bloomington, MN.
2. Steve Benson, personal interview with the author, February 9, 2011, Minneapolis, MN.
3. Benson, interview.

Chapter One: A Long Legacy of Trouble

4. Quoted in Norway!, "Trolls in Norway." www.2beinnorway.com.
5. Joanne Asala, *Norwegian Troll Tales*. Iowa City, IA: Penfield, 2005, p. 7.
6. Florence Ekstrand, *Norwegian Trolls and Other Tales*. Seattle: Welcome, 1990, pp. 14–15.
7. Asala, *Norwegian Troll Tales*, p. 9.
8. Ekstrand, *Norwegian Trolls and Other Tales*, p. 25.
9. Quoted in Peter Asbjornsen and Jorgen Moe, *Norwegian Folk Tales*, trans. Pat Shaw and Carl Norman. New York: Pantheon, 1982, p. 70.
10. Benson, interview.
11. Ekstrand, *Norwegian Trolls and Other Tales*, p. 26.
12. Ekstrand, *Norwegian Trolls and Other Tales*, p. 27.
13. Quoted in Rootsweb, "The Norwegian Folk Tales and Their Illustrators." www.rootsweb.ancestry.com.
14. Ekstrand, *Norwegian Trolls and Other Tales*, p. 29.
15. John Lindow, *Swedish Legends and Folktales*. Berkeley: University of California Press, 1978, p. 33.
16. Benson, interview.
17. Benson, interview.
18. Ekstrand, *Norwegian Trolls and Other Tales*, p. 20.

Chapter Two: Bloodthirsty, Vicious, and Slow

19. Ekstrand, *Norwegian Trolls and Other Tales*, p. 34.

20. Norwegian Folktales, "Dyre Vaa," 2009. http://oaks.nvg.org.

21. Quoted in Norwegian Folktales, "Dyre Vaa."

22. Quoted in William A. Craigie, ed. and trans., *Scandinavian Folk-Lore: Illustrations of the Traditional Beliefs of the Northern Peoples*. London: A. Gardner, 1909, pp. 62–63.

23. Craigie, *Scandinavian Folk-Lore*, p. 63.

24. Quoted in Asala, *Norwegian Troll Tales*, p. 24.

25. Asbjornsen and Moe, *Norwegian Folk Tales*, p. 10.

26. Quoted in Asala, *Norwegian Troll Tales*, p. 25.

27. Quoted in Ekstrand, *Norwegian Trolls and Other Tales*, p. 38.

28. Ekstrand, *Norwegian Trolls and Other Tales*, p. 38.

29. Ekstrand, *Norwegian Trolls and Other Tales*, p. 101.

30. Quoted in Ekstrand, *Norwegian Trolls and Other Tales*, p. 101.

31. Quoted in Ekstrand, *Norwegian Trolls and Other Tales*, p. 101.

32. Benson, interview.

33. Asala, *Norwegian Troll Tales*, p. 101.

34. Quoted in Asala, *Norwegian Troll Tales*, p. 102.

35. Quoted in Asala, *Norwegian Troll Tales*, p. 146.

36. Quoted in Asala, *Norwegian Troll Tales*, p. 146.

37. Quoted in Asala, *Norwegian Troll Tales*, p. 147.

38. Quoted in Lise Lunge-Larsen, *The Troll with No Heart in His Body and Other Tales of Trolls from Norway*. Boston: Houghton Mifflin, 1999, p. 73.

39. Quoted in Lunge-Larsen, *The Troll with No Heart in His Body*, p. 73.

Chapter Three: The Troll Family Tree

40. Ekstrand, *Norwegian Trolls and Other Tales*, p. 48.

41. Quoted in Asala, *Norwegian Troll Tales*, p. 110.

42. Quoted in Craigie, *Scandinavian Folk-Lore*, p. 113.

43. Quoted in Asala, *Norwegian Troll Tales*, pp. 129–130.

44. Joanne Asala, *Trolls Remembering Norway: Stories and History*. Iowa City, IA: Penfield, 1994, p. 128.

45. Ekstrand, *Norwegian Trolls and Other Tales*, p. 52.

46. Knutsen, interview.

47. Craigie, *Scandinavian Folk-Lore*, p. 191.

48. Ekstrand, *Norwegian Trolls and Other Tales*, p. 45.

49. Quoted in Craigie, *Scandinavian Folk-Lore*, p. 197.

50. Craigie, *Scandinavian Folk-Lore*, p. 197.

51. Knutsen, interview.

52. Knutsen, interview.

Chapter Four: Beyond the Early Legends

53. Henrik Ibsen, *Peer Gynt: A Dramatic Poem*, trans. Christopher Fry and Johan Fillinger. New York: Oxford University Press, 1998, p. 26.

54. Quoted in Asala, *Trolls Remembering Norway*, pp. 92–93.

55. Ibsen, *Peer Gynt*, p. 41.

56. Quoted in Asala, *Trolls Remembering Norway*, p. 85.

57. Quoted in Anthony Tommasini, "Respect at Last for Grieg?," *New York Times*, September 16, 2007. www.nytimes.com.

58. J.R.R. Tolkien, *The Hobbit; or There, and Back Again*. Boston: Houghton Mifflin, 1996, p. 31.

59. Tolkien, *The Hobbit*, pp. 31–32.

60. Tolkien, *The Hobbit*, p. 38.

61. J.K. Rowling, *Harry Potter and the Sorcerer's Stone*. New York: Scholastic, 1997, p. 174.

62. Rowling, *Harry Potter*, p. 174.

63. Jerry Shapiro, telephone interview with author, March 30, 2011.

64. Quoted in Lisa Belkin, "An Internet Star's Mom Responds," *New York Times*, March 25, 2011. http://parenting.blogs.ny times.com.

65. Quoted in Joshua Gillin, "Rebecca Black Feels 'Cyberbullied' by 'Friday' Trolls," *St. Petersburg (FL) Times*, March 18, 2011. www.tampabay.com.

66. Knutsen, interview.

67. Lunge-Larsen, *The Troll with No Heart in His Body and Other Tales of Trolls from Norway*, pp. 9–10.

68. Lise Lunge-Larsen, telephone interview with author, March 22, 2011.

For Further Exploration

Books

Joanne Asala, *Norwegian Troll Tales*. Iowa City, IA: Penfield, 2010.

Ingri d'Aulaire and Edgar Parin d'Aulaire, *D'Aulaires' Book of Trolls*. New York: New York Review, 2006.

Lone Thygesen Blecher and George Blecher, eds. and trans., *Swedish Folktales and Legends*. Minneapolis: University of Minnesota Press, 2004.

Henrik Ibsen, *Peer Gynt: A Dramatic Poem*. Translated by Christopher Fry and Johan Fillinger. New York: Oxford University Press, 1998.

Elsa Olenius, ed., and Holger Lundbergh, trans., *Swedish Fairy Tales*. New York: Skyhorse, 2010.

Websites

The Gold Scales (http://oaks.nvg.org/norwegian-folktales.html). This site contains more than 200 folktales from Norway, Iceland, Sweden, Finland, and Denmark—many of them featuring trolls and troll relatives.

John Bauer Art (http://bauer.artpassions.net). This site includes not only colorful images of Bauer's best-known work, but also a biography of the artist. There are links to dozens of black-and-white drawings depicting various folktales.

Myths of the Norsemen (www.munseys.com/diskseven/mynodex.htm). This site provides intricate, detailed background on some of the trolls (called "giants" here) as well as some of the background of their hostility toward churches and church bells.

Theodor Kittelsen (http://kittelsen.efenstor.net/index.php). Here are scores of Kittelsen's drawings, many of which were used in volumes about trolls, and others depicting the bleak landscape of the Norwegian mountain area with which he was so familiar.

Trolls: Culture and Development (http://ccb.lis.illinois.edu/Projects/storytelling/jvmccaff/intro1.html). This site would be helpful to anyone doing a school report on trolls. It contains basic background information, as well as sections on how to defeat a troll, the various types of trolls, troll family life, and troll magic.

Index

Note: Boldface page numbers indicate illustrations.

Picture Credits

About the Author

Gail B. Stewart is the author of more than 260 books for teens and young adults. The mother of three sons, she lives with her husband in Minneapolis, Minnesota.